Billy Bloo
Is Stuck in GOO

by JENNIFER HAMBURG

illustrations by ROSS BURACH

Scholastic Press • New York

WHATEVER YOU DO...
DO NOT
GO IN THE
GOO!

For Mathis, Hazel, and Jeremy. May none of you get stuck in goo. —JH

For Dad, my emergency contact if I'm ever stuck in goo. —RB

Library of Congress Cataloging-in-Publication Data available

ISBN 978-0-545-88015-2

10 9 8 7 6 5 4 3 2 1   17 18 19 20 21

Printed in China   62
First edition, August 2017

The display type was set in Ranchers Regular.
The text type was set in 18 point BernhardGothicSG Medium.
The art was created using digital media.

Book design by Marijka Kostiw

This is Billy. Billy Bloo.

Billy Bloo is stuck in goo.

Who will help him, tell me who?

Who'll unstick him from this goo?

Would you?

"**Yeeeehaw,**

I'll git you out real fast!"
declares a cowgirl riding past!

She spins her rope 'round Billy's shin.
Then loses grip . . .

and falls right in!

Billy Bloo, still stuck in goo.
And now the cowgirl's stuck there too.

What would you do?

"BEHOLD!

Our acrobatic troupe
will pull you from this gooey goop.
We promise, it will be a breeze.
We even brought our own trapeze!"

They clutch the bar. They sling it back.
Then in midswing, they hear a

Four acrobats, the cowgirl too,
and sadly, still, poor Billy Bloo.
The lot of them are stuck in goo.

Just who'll unstick them now?

Would you?

"AHOY,

The POLLY PiRate

me mateys, take a look!
You're stuck in goo?
I have a hook!"

They think the hook will help — instead . . .

the pirate plops in on his head.

Have any butter?

Four acrobats, the cowgirl too,
the pirate, and poor Billy Bloo —
quite a few now stuck in goo.

What would you do?

"TADA!

Your friendly wizard here!
And through my wizardly career,
    I've learned to make things disappear!
    I'll do that with this goo right here!
(No need to beg. I volunteer!)"

AWAK!
AWOOK!
ADOOBLY DOO!

"Egads! It seems I've made more goo."

Four acrobats, the cowgirl too,
the pirate, and poor Billy Bloo —
and now a puzzled wizard, who
has somehow made TWO TIMES MORE GOO.
So many stuck now. What to do?
Who will rescue them?

Would you?

"Hey, dudes!

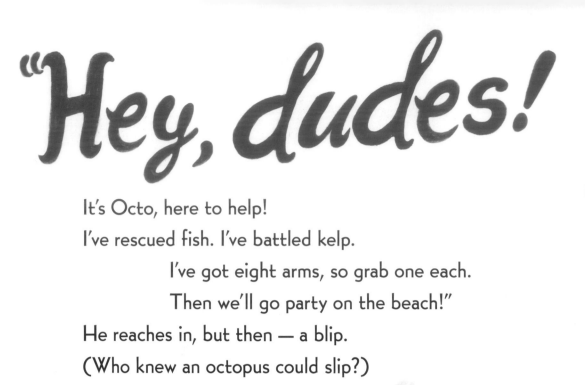

It's Octo, here to help!
I've rescued fish. I've battled kelp.
I've got eight arms, so grab one each.
Then we'll go party on the beach!"
He reaches in, but then — a blip.
(Who knew an octopus could slip?)

Four acrobats, the cowgirl too,
the pirate, wizard, Billy Bloo —
plus now an octopus, it's true.
All of them are . . .

DOO DOO DOO!

"Hear Ye!

It is I, the queen!
I've come to do a queenly thing!

My nobles, seventeen in all,
will get you out, and they won't stall!"
The nobles take a flying leap —

but end up in a gooey heap.
Four acrobats, the cowgirl too,
the octopus, the wizard (who
just conjured up a talking ewe),
the pirate, and the noble crew.
(And by the way, the queen's there too,
though, how that happened? Not a clue.)

By now, it really isn't clear
that Billy will get out of here.
    As gobs of goo go squish and splat,
    he feels it's time to have a chat.
"Dear friends, how very kind of you
to try and get me out of goo.
    I do admire all your pluck.
    Just thought I'd point out . . .

I'M STILL STUCK!!!"

The others spring to his defense.
(They do not want things to get tense.)

"I'll use my rope!"

"We'll swing some more!"

"I'll call my friend
the dinosaur!"

The talking ewe
is now part cat.

KAZEEM!
KAZOOM!
KAZOWIE...ZAT!

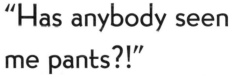

"Unruly goo, you stand
NO chance!"

"Has anybody seen
me pants?!"

They push, they pull, they squeeze, they jerk.
They dance a jig (it doesn't work).
 "I guess that's it," says Billy Bloo.
 "Get used to living in this goo.
There's nothing more that we can do,
unless a miracle —"

achoo

A tiny mouse then scampers by,
and catches Octo's watchful eye.
That's all it takes, one sneezy squeak.
The octopus says simply . . .

EEEEEEEEK!!

He leaps out from the gooey goop,
and snags the acrobatic troupe,
who grab the cowgirl and the queen,
who nabs her crew, all seventeen,
who lift the pirate, wizard too,
and last but not least, Billy Bloo,
who **FINALLY** is out of goo.

But look, oh no, he lost his shoe.

This is Billy. Billy Bloo.
The only one not stuck in goo.

What would you do?